Rabbit /
599.32 BUT
Butterfield, Moira,
COLUMBIA SCHOOL MEDIA CENTER

BORROWER'S NAME | ROOM NUMBER

Rabbit /
599.32 BUT
Butterfield, Moira,
COLUMBIA SCHOOL MEDIA CENTER

COLUMBIA SCHOOL MEDIA CENTER

WHO AM I?

Who am I?

Titles in the series

Black-and-White (Panda)
Furry and Fluffy-tailed (Rabbit)
Long-necked and Lean   (Giraffe)
Winged and Wild (Golden Eagle)

I am furry and fluffy-tailed, small and soft.
I live in a burrow.

WHO AM I?

By Moira Butterfield
Illustrated by Wayne Ford

Thameside Press

US publication copyright © Thameside Press.
International copyright reserved in all countries.
No part of this book may be reproduced in any form
without written permission from the publisher.

Distributed in the United States by
Smart Apple Media
1980 Lookout Drive
North Mankato, MN 56003

ISBN 1-930643-93-4

Library of Congress Control Number 2002 141347

Printed by South China Printing Co. Ltd., Hong Kong

Editor: Stephanie Bellwood
Designer: Helen James
Illustrator: Wayne Ford / Wildlife Art Agency
Consultant: Steve Pollock

My ears are long.
My fur is brown.
I live in burrows underground.
I like to hop around for fun,
But if I see a fox I'll run.

Who am I?

Here is my eye.

I use my eyes
to look for food.
I eat grass and
juicy plant stems.

Now and then I look
around for enemies.
This owl would like
to swoop down and
catch me for dinner.

Here is my fur.

My fur is soft and brown. It keeps me dry and warm. I lick it to keep it clean.

Sometimes I leave tiny bits of fur on bushes as I run past. Birds take the fur to put in their nests.

Here is my tail.

My tail is very short. The fur on top is brown and the fur underneath is white.

You can see the white part of my tail as I disappear into my burrow.

Here are my legs.

I use my front paws to dig tunnels in the ground. I have long claws on each paw.

My back legs are strong. I can run very fast. I also use my back legs to kick enemies.

Here are my ears.

I can hear sounds
all around me.
I listen for enemies.
Can you see any?

I stay close to other
animals like me.
If we hear an
enemy, we run
back to our warren.

Here are my teeth.

My front teeth are long and strong. I use them for cutting plant stems. My back teeth are flat for grinding my food.

Sometimes I go into farmland to eat the plants. I like to nibble cabbage leaves.

Here is my nose.

I twitch my nose to pick up smells in the air. If I smell, hear, or see an enemy I warn all my friends.

I drum my back feet on the ground...
thump, thump, thump!

Have you guessed who I am?

I am a rabbit.

Point to my…

strong back legs

soft fur

short tail

round eye

front paws

twitchy nose

long ears

I am called an
Old World rabbit.

Here are my babies.

They are called kittens. I look after them in my burrow. I make a cozy bed with bits of my fur.

When my babies grow bigger and stronger they come out of the burrow and play outside.

Here is my territory.

I live in fields or woods, or on heaths.

How many rabbits can you count? Can you see four butterflies, two other insects, and a blackbird catching a worm?

Here is a map of the world.

I live in lots of different countries. Can you see the places where I live?

Can you point to the place where you live?

South Ameri

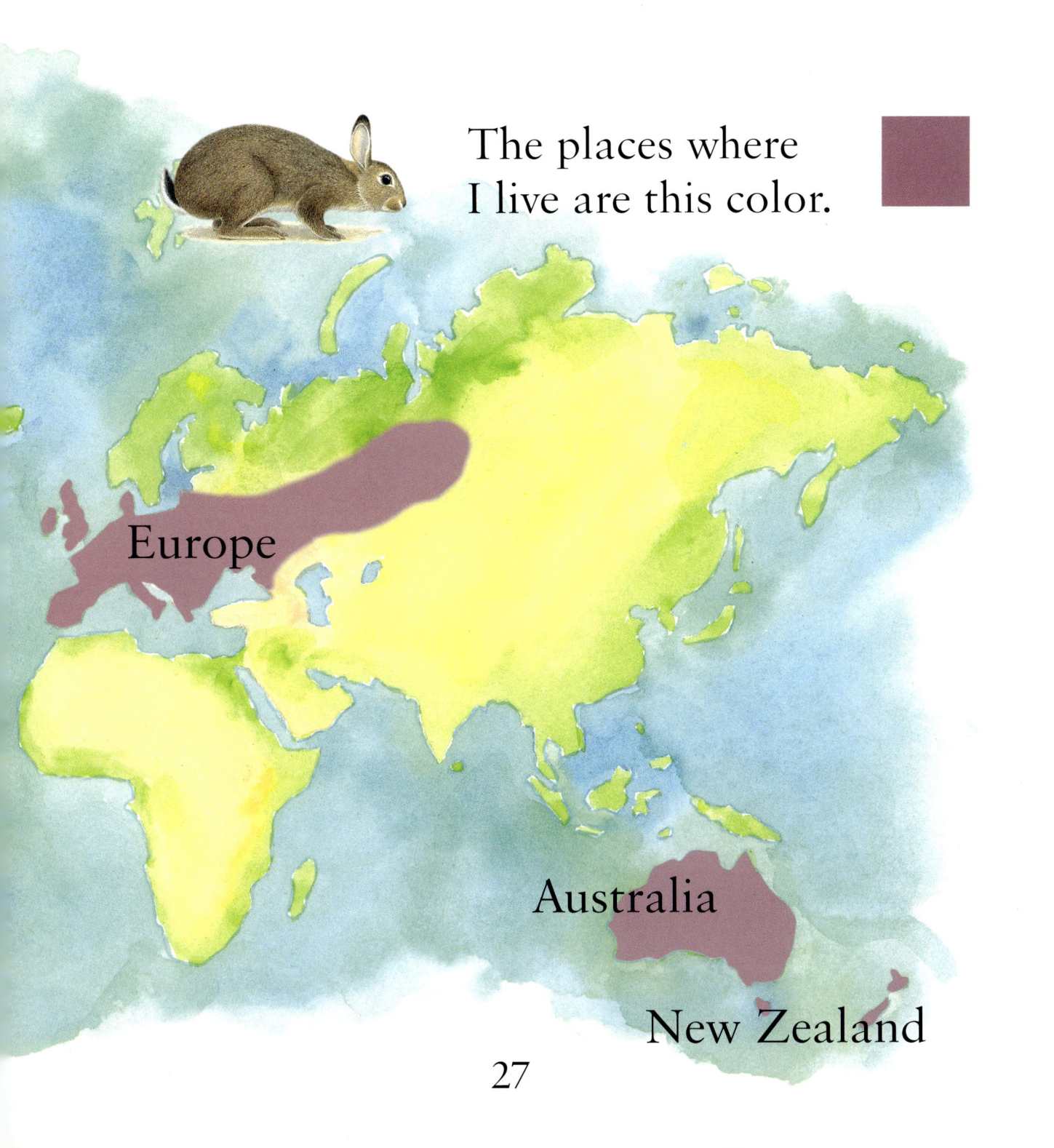

The places where
I live are this color.

Europe

Australia

New Zealand

Can you answer these questions about me?

What do I like to eat?

What is the name of my underground home?

Who are my enemies?

What are my babies called?

What color
is my tail when
I hold it up?

How do I clean my fur?

How do I know if
an enemy is near?

What do I use
my paws for?

Here are some words to learn about me.

burrow A tunnel that I dig in the ground. Many rabbits dig burrows near each other. A group of burrows is called a warren.

claws The long, sharp nails on my paws.

enemy An animal that tries to catch me and eat me.

grinding Chewing something into small pieces. I grind food with my back teeth.

heath A large, open area of rough land.

kitten The name for a baby rabbit.

territory The area around my warren. I share my territory with many other rabbits. We come out of our warren in the evening or at night to look for food.

twitch A quick movement. I twitch my nose to sniff the air. Can you twitch your nose?

warren All the tunnels that make up my home. Other rabbits live in the warren too.

INDEX

babies 22-3, 31
birds' nests 9
blackbird 25
burrows 5, 23, 30
butterflies 25
claws 13, 30
cleaning 9
digging 13
ears 5, 14-15
enemies 7, 13, 15, 19, 30
eyes 6–7
farmland 17
food 7, 17
fox 5
fur 5, 8–9, 11, 23

grinding 17, 30
heath 24, 31
home 5
insects 25
kittens 22–3, 31
legs 12–13

map of world 26–7
nose 18–19
owl 7
questions 28–9
rabbit 20–1
smell 19
tail 10–11
teeth 16–17
territory 24–5, 31
tunnels 13, 30, 31
twitch 19, 31
warning noise 19
warren 15, 30, 31
washing 9
world map 26–7